ANIMORPHS

THE INVASION

ORPHS
THE INVASION

K.A. APPLEGATE & **MICHAEL GRANT**
A GRAPHIC NOVEL BY **CHRIS GRINE**

graphix
An Imprint of
📖 SCHOLASTIC

All rights reserved. Published by Graphix, an imprint of Scholastic Inc.,
Publishers since 1920. SCHOLASTIC, GRAPHIX, ANIMORPHS, and associated
logos are trademarks and/or registered trademarks of Scholastic Inc.

The publisher does not have any control over and does not assume any
responsibility for author or third-party websites or their content.

Library of Congress Control Number Available

ISBN 978-1-338-22648-5 (hardcover)
ISBN 978-1-338-53809-0 (paperback)

10 9 8 7 6 5 4 3 2 1   20 21 22 23 24

Printed in China   62
First edition, October 2020
Edited by Zack Clark
Book design by Phil Falco
Publisher: David Saylor

For Ani-fans everywhere.
You're the best fandom ever.
–KAA & MR

For Robyn, who could clearly
see what she was getting into but
married me anyway.
–CG

WE CAN'T TELL YOU OUR LAST NAMES.

IT WOULD BE **TOO** DANGEROUS.

THE CONTROLLERS ARE EVERYWHERE.

EVERYWHERE.

5

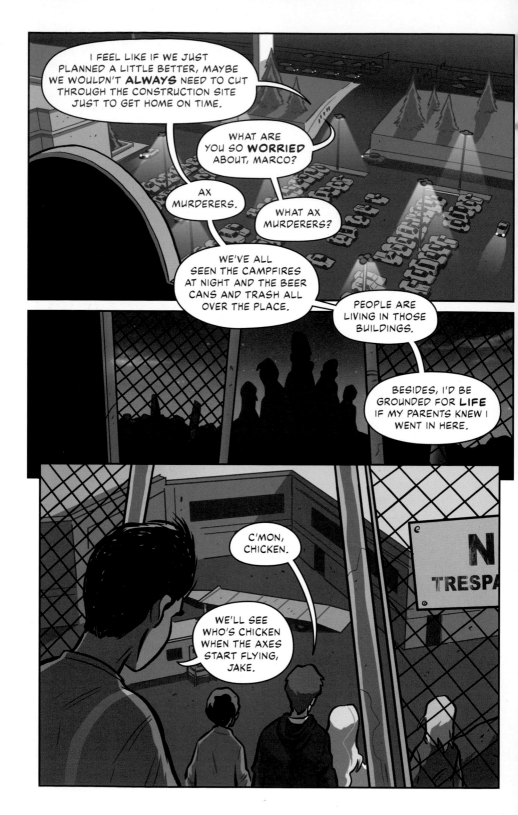

14

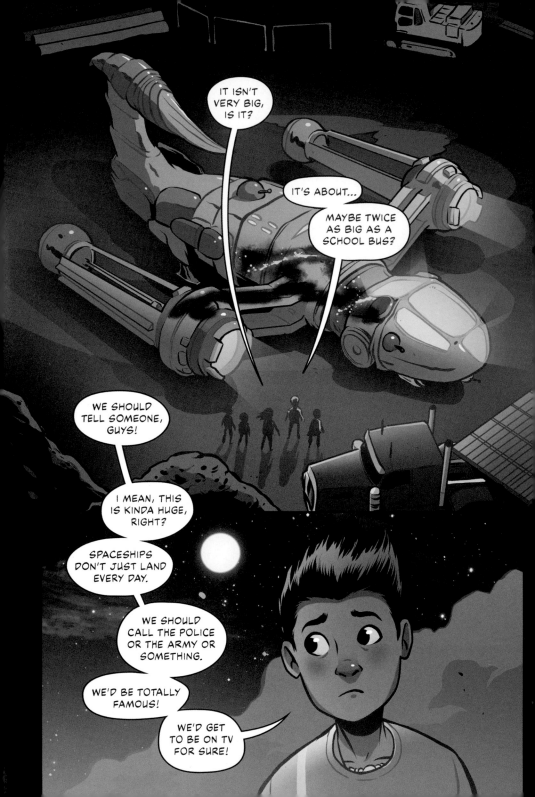

34

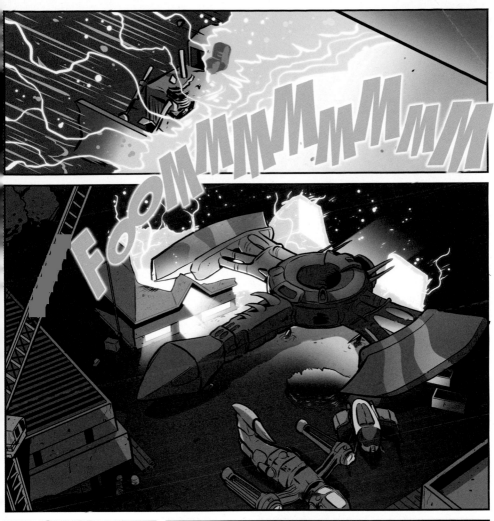

FOOMMMMMMM

THOSE CONSTRUCTION GUYS AREN'T GONNA BE HAPPY ABOUT THAT.

THE DOORS ARE OPENING, GUYS.

WE NEED TO *GO!*

43

47

59

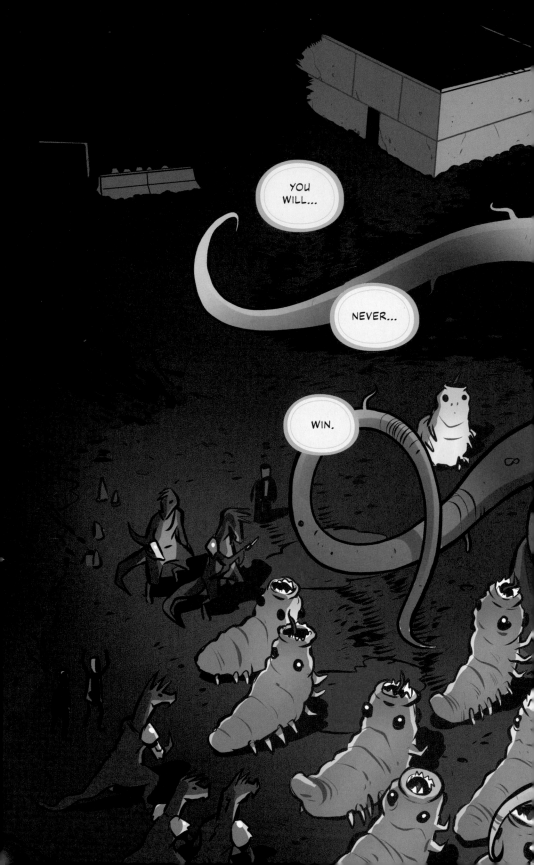

64

65

FUR. I HAD **FUR!**

AND I WAS GROWING CLAWS.

DUDE **FREAKED** OUT!

I HAD TO PUT HIM OUTSIDE BEFORE I MORPHED ALL THE WAY.

HE CLAWED ME UP PRETTY GOOD.

TOBIAS, ARE YOU SURE YOU WEREN'T MAYBE JUST DREAMING ALL THIS?

IT WASN'T A DREAM.

IT'S REAL, JAKE. **ALL** OF IT.

I CAN'T DESCRIBE WHAT IT WAS LIKE BEING A CAT.

YOU'RE SO STRONG. LIKE COILED-UP POWER READY TO EXPLODE.

AND THE WAY YOU CAN **MOVE!**

I JUMPED ONTO MY DRESSER! FOUR FEET STRAIGHT UP AND I LANDED LIKE A FEATHER.

I KEPT CONCENTRATING, AND IN A FEW MINUTES...

I WASN'T... MYSELF ANYMORE.

93

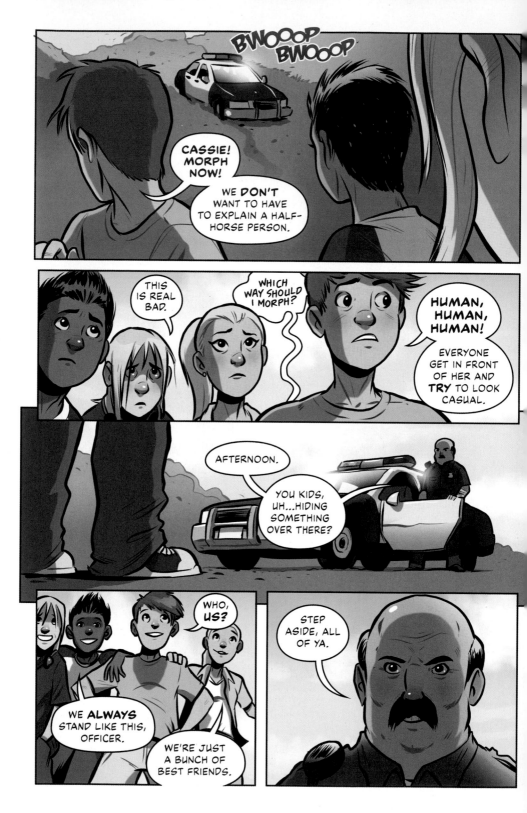

I HAVEN'T SORTED IT OUT YET...

HOLD ON TO THAT THOUGHT.

LET ME CHECK THE DOOR.

ALL CLEAR.

IT'S TOM.

HE'S ONE OF THEM.

WHAT'S... GOING ON?

DON'T START THAT CONTROLLER STUFF AGAIN, MARCO.

EITHER WAY, WE SHOULD BE MORE CAREFUL.

OKAY, SO THE KANDRONA'S LIKE A PORTABLE VERSION OF THE YEERK'S SUN. IT MAKES THE PARTICLES THAT THEY NEED TO SURVIVE, AND BEAMS THEM TO THESE POOLS.

EVERY THREE DAYS THE YEERKS LEAVE THEIR HOSTS TO VISIT THE POOL AND SOAK UP THE PARTICLES.

THEN...THEY RETURN TO THEIR HOSTS.

AND SO YOU THOUGHT THEY WOULD JUST LEAVE THEIR ALIEN WORM POOLS OUT IN THE OPEN?

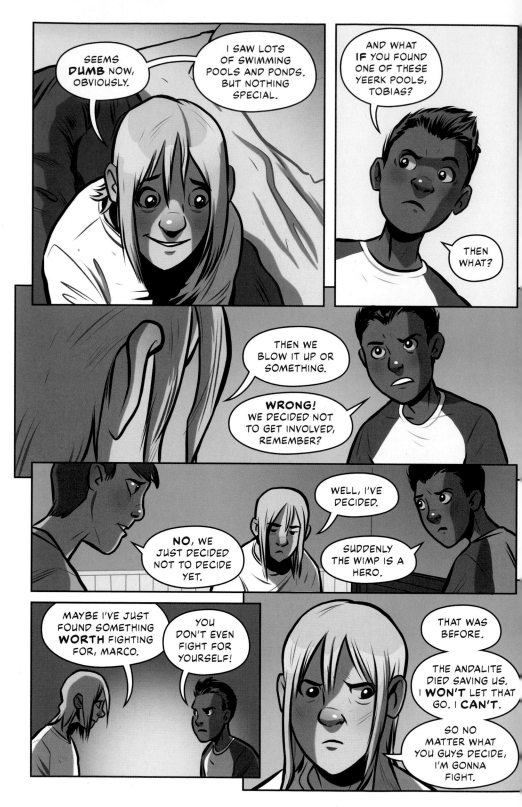

LATER THAT DAY...

IT'S THE YEERK POOL. I'M **SURE** OF IT.

I CAN'T STAND THE THOUGHT OF WHAT'S HAPPENING TO PEOPLE DOWN THERE. IT'S SICKENING.

So Much CHEESE

YOU WERE A LIZARD AT THE TIME. WHO KNOWS **WHAT** YOU HEARD.

I **KNOW** WHAT I HEARD, MARCO. IT WAS PEOPLE.

WE HAVE TO DO SOMETHING.

YEAH, LET'S RUSH RIGHT DOWN THERE SO IT CAN BE **US** SCREAMING.

141

145

191

203

K.A. APPLEGATE is the married writing team Katherine Applegate and Michael Grant. Their Animorphs™ series has sold millions of copies worldwide and alerted the world to the presence of the Yeerks. Katherine is also the author of the Endling series and the Newbery Medal–winning *The One and Only Ivan*. Michael is also the author of the Front Lines and Gone series.

CHRIS GRINE is the creator of Chickenhare and *Time Shifters*. He's been making up stories since he was a kid, and not just to get out of trouble with his parents. Nowadays, Chris spends most of his time writing and illustrating books, drinking lots of coffee, and sleeping as little as possible. He spends his free time with his wife, playing with his kids, watching movies, and collecting action figures (but only the bad guys).

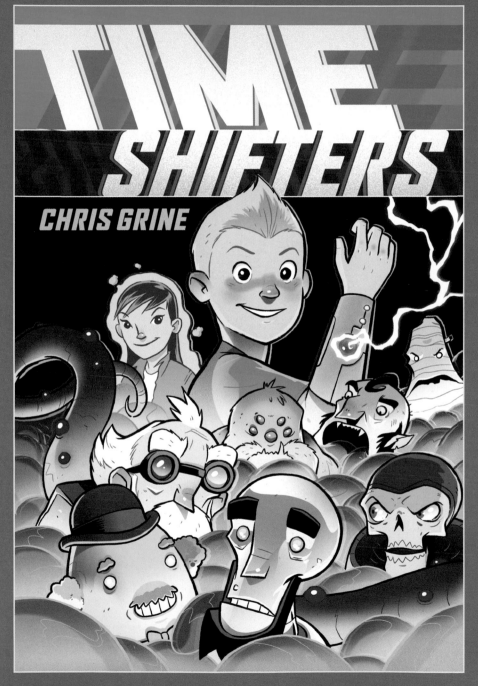

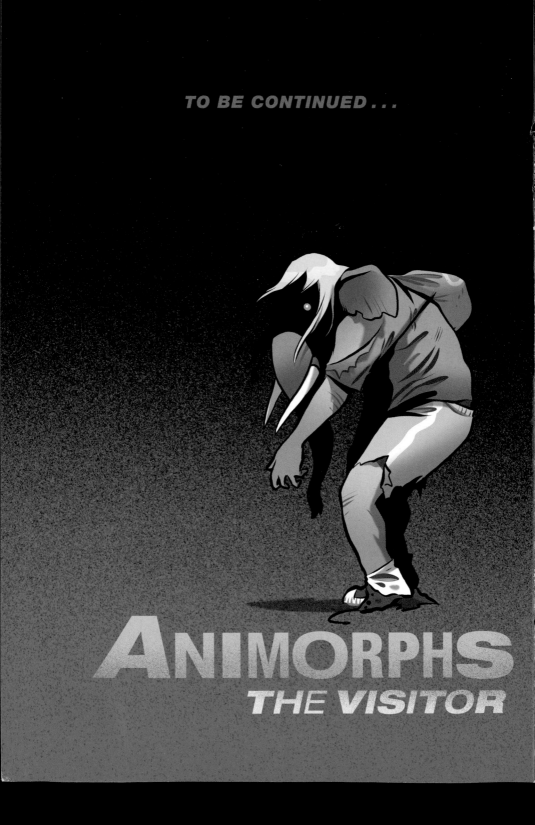

TO BE CONTINUED...

ANIMORPHS
THE VISITOR